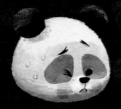

For those on the road to chasing dreams
—Y.L.

FENNIE

Ying Li

Chapter 1

Secret

Ding-ding-ding, school was over,
all the students were ready to go home.

Usually, Fennie went home together with her friends Koala and Panda. But today, she stayed and had something else to do.

Fennie went to the music classroom quietly.
She heard that the choir was rehearsing
a beautiful song, and she wanted to learn it.

Outside the window of the music classroom, she was deeply attracted by the singing of the choir.

The guitar club would have an activity soon. As the president, Ricky arrived on time.

Staring at his back enviously, Fennie desired to pursue her dreams as bravely as he did.

After the choir rehearsal, Fennie was going to leave while she noticed the little Mia sitting on the rest chair depressedly. So Fennie kindly walked toward her and asked what happened.

It turned out this was Mia's first school day, but she didn't make any new friend due to her shyness.

In order to delight Mia, Fennie took out her favorite candies and shared with her. Mia was finally happy again.

They enjoyed the happy moment and sweet candies.

After that, Fennie gently sent Mia onto the school bus. But Fennie didn't leave, since she had a secret "little plan"......

Passing through the pretty woods
and quiet grass hills behind the school,
Fennie stopped by the crystal clear stream.

After returning the inner peace,
she cleared the throat......

Facing the graceful nature, she let go herself
and started to sing loudly and freely.
Her beautiful voice sounded as if full of magic,
fusing everything around her into a wonderful melody.

Fennie was very excited and
relaxed every time she sang alone.
This was her own secret.

No one knew her love of singing,

and no one had ever heard her unique singing.

Sometimes she hoped to sing bravely like others,

but her shyness kept her from stepping forward.

On the way home,
Fennie passed by the flower
shop run by Panda's father.

She gave them the wild flowers picked at the riverside as a gift.

Finally, it's home, the best stage to free her love of singing.

In the music class the next day,
the Giraffe teacher asked everyone to
sing solely. Fennie was so nervous at
the thought of singing in front of everyone.

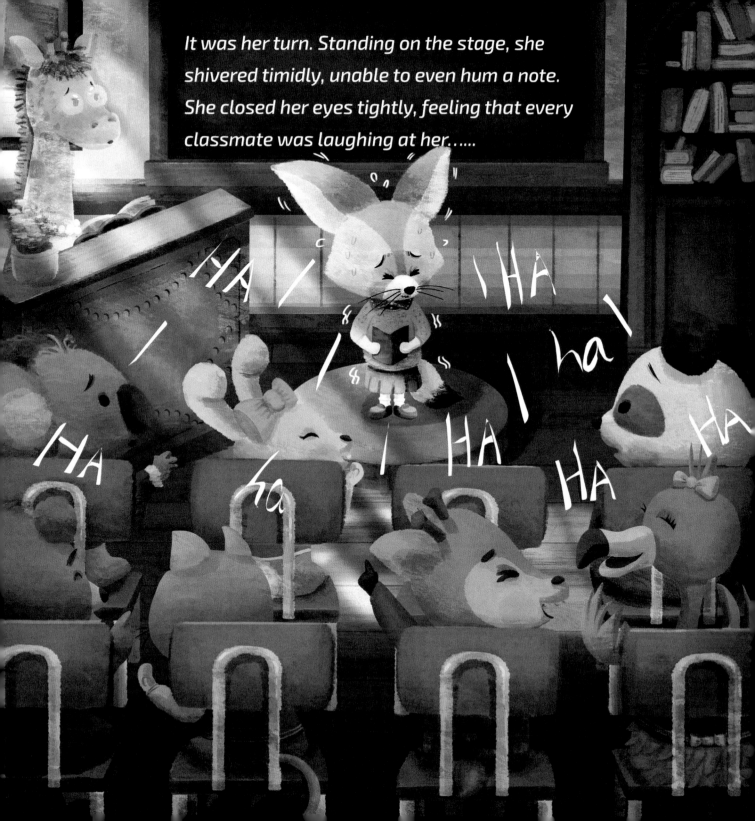

It was her turn. Standing on the stage, she shivered timidly, unable to even hum a note. She closed her eyes tightly, feeling that every classmate was laughing at her......

After the music class, Koala and Panda tried to appease Fennie who was trapped in self-blame and frustration.

How desired she wanted everyone
to know about her love of singing!

Being a singer is her dream!

Chapter 2

Surprise

At the weekend, Fennie and her friends decided
to help Panda's father gather fresh flowers.
They drove to the flower farm cheerfully.

Everyone was working energetically,
and Panda's father smiled from ear to ear.
what a meaningful day!

In the charming sea of flowers, Fennie was fascinated and couldn't help humming an enchanting melody.

Friends were all attracted by her sweet singing. They had never heard it before.

After Fennie finished the song, friends applauded sincerely.
Only then did she realize that everyone was listening,
and their enthusiastic feedback surprised her.

Fennie's friends firmly believed
that she would become an excellent
singer one day!

After classes on Monday, Koala and Panda brought a singing competition flyer to Fennie and encouraged her to participate.

After school, she walked home anxiously.

When she passed by the flower shop as usual,

Panda's father kindly invited her to the shop,

which made her a little confused......

She opened the door slowly
and looked inside curiously.
What was waiting for her?

To make Fennie's dream possible, her friends decided to be her band, even though Mia and Koala had never learned musical instruments before. Luckily, Ricky and Panda would ramp them up.

Fennie was so moved by everything happening.
She never thought her friends were so supportive.
With their encouragement, she decided
to be brave and challenge herself.

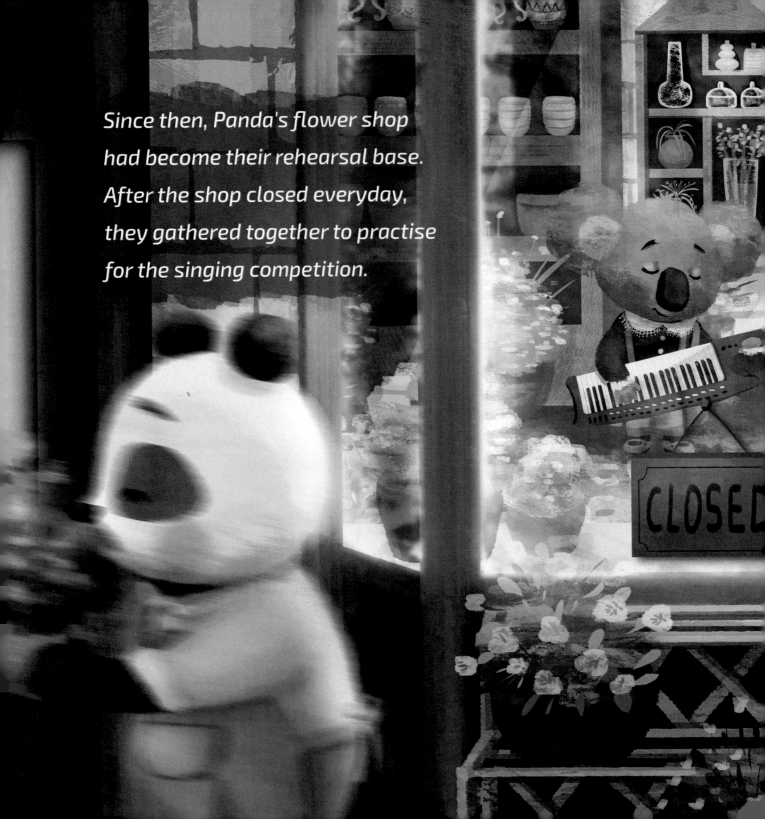

Since then, Panda's flower shop had become their rehearsal base. After the shop closed everyday, they gathered together to practise for the singing competition.

Chapter 3
Surmount

Time flew, it was the day of competition. It seemed that every contestant was full of confidence, except Fennie, who was in extreme anxiety and tension.

When she was at a loss,
her friends arrived, which
calmed Fennie down quickly.

Panda's father brought her a piece of four-leaf clover
symbolizing faith, hope, love and luck, and wished her all the best.

Fennie and her friends waited anxiously in the backstage. The ongoing performance was pretty excellent, which made them stressed but motivated.

It was their turn next!

Finally, the moment came.
Fennie stood at the center of the stage
with friends behind.

All the spotlights and eyes
were focusing on them.

To relax her, Ricky gently pulled her ear as a reminder like before.

Looking at Ricky holding a victory sign, Fennie gained confidence again from the encouragement of friends.

The performance eventually began!

It was the first time Fennie broke through herself and sang bravely in front of so many audiences. All are attracted deeply by her fantastic singing.

Her performance was remarkable
and a great success.

At that moment, Fennie and her friends felt that all their efforts paid off.

After all the performances, the audience was going to vote for their favorite singers.

The singer who got the most votes would be the **champion!**

  "And now, the most exciting

moment is coming..."

"who is the champion ???!!!"

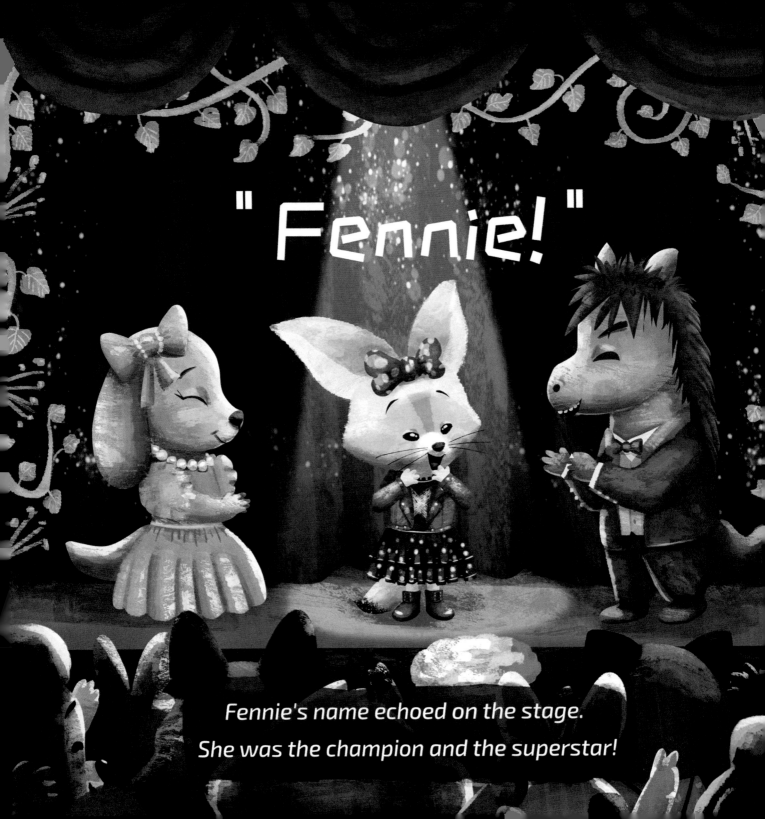

"Fennie!"

Fennie's name echoed on the stage.

She was the champion and the superstar!

Fennie invited her
friends onto the stage
to share the honor.

This trophy stood
for a dream built
by friendship and
courage.

Since then, Fennie was no longer timid and hesitated, because she knew whenever and wherever, there were always reliable pals behind.

THE END

About the Author

Ying Li is a freelance writer and illustrator mainly focusing on children's books.
She lives in California, US.

Find out more interesting stories about Fennie and her friends at

 @Fennecthefoxandfriends

Follow the author:

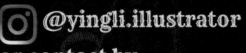 @yingli.illustrator @Ying Li

or contact by

 yingli315cn@gmail.com

Made in the USA
Coppell, TX
24 November 2024

40880493R00048